TerraMars:
A Ranger's Honor

Drew H. Justis

Drew H. Justis

Copyright © 2020 Drew H. Justis

All rights reserved.

ISBN: 9798646745485
ISBN-13:

DEDICATION

To all those who enjoy space, know that one day our dreams will lead us to the stars.

Drew H. Justis

5

ACKNOWLEDGMENTS

To those who explore the final frontier

CHAPTER 1
TRADE

10/20/2300

I suppose I should have seen it coming. Juliett is the most junior team present so it was a given that we'd be given whatever job nobody else wanted. Still I had hoped that when the Argonaut docked with the main orbital station, very close to the ranger command station, that we would get to go down to Mars. The Argonaut had taken a bit of a beating and would need repairs, and on top of that it still needed to unload it's cargo. Under normal circumstances the cargo would take weeks to get through customs and would take several days to deliver them down to the planet. Luckily for the princess the cargo side of things would be easy. One of the first things some of the other teams had done when we arrived was to conduct a full inspection of the cargo and the ship. This was done in the name of defence as well as to relieve boredom. The Earthlings hadn't taken too kindly to the unexpected inspection but their princess had decreed that we would be allowed to do so. After getting to know her a little I strongly suspect she had done so, fully knowing her crew would be displeased, just to get around customs. As I had suspected, the very first thing she did when we arrived in orbit was to transmit our inspection to customs and asked to immediately be allowed to begin unloading her cargo.

I had enjoyed watching the rangers in charge of customs, good men and women one and all but they tend to have a stick up their asses, slowly realizing they won't have anything to do. Like must rangers they must have been excited at the prospect of a job to do, hunting for contraband in their case, but they could hardly do an inspection now that it's clear we had done our own. I'd be willing to bet the rangers in charge of the inspection would have been willing to go through with the inspection anyway but we all had been told to be extra nice with this particular ship so they just asked for the standard docking fee before directing us to an open docking port. After a brief discussion about repair costs the Argonaut docked with the main orbital station and the crew began loading the containers onto their cargo shuttles. The other teams were preparing to leave and go visit family, bury the dead, just get away from the Earthlings for a short time. Thora had said we'd be here for a month before leaving so we had plenty of time to enjoy ourselves but just as I was about to leave with my half of the team and join the others in the hanger the princess asked if we'd be willing to provide an escort for her.

"I'm sorry but, why would you need an escort?" It's our job to deal with trade and anyone needing saving in our small section of space. Escorting somebody planetside isn't part of the job description and I know she's aware of that.

"I have a meeting with some representatives from the United Kingdom Kingdom Dome and figured having a ranger to guide us around would make things easier." The British dome?

"Not sure what you want there but it has nothing to do with rangers. If you'll excuse me, I need to meet with the rest of my team." She didn't look too happy about being told no, but then again I hardly cared. I have been rather nice to her and I felt we had gotten off well enough but that doesn't mean I'm going to step outside my bounds for her. As I made my way down to the hanger though Lucas came on the radio.

"Abelus, command wants an escort for the princess's away team. I took the liberty of nominating you." What the hell?

"Come again?"

"You. Escorting the princess. Need the orders in writing?"

"May I ask why a ranger is supposed to be pulling escort groundside?" And why I have to be the one to do it.

"Apparently the princess is a VIP, who'd have thought that? Command doesn't want anything happening to her and when she raised concerns about security, command was quick to offer her a ranger to guard her." Oh for the love of…

"May I ask why I've been given this particular honor?"

"No reason." I thought about this for a moment before responding. What did I do to get on his bad side?

"And your decision to volunteer me had nothing to do with the amount of money you owe me after last night's poker tournament?"

"Nothing at all. Just thought that among all of us you had the best relationship with the princess." Sure…

"In that case you'll have the money you owe me when I get back?" I wait for a minute but I don't get a response. Turning to the others I motion them on ahead while I head back to the bridge. I had already restocked my ammo and had lunch earlier so there was no reason for me to go back to the hanger. With a simple nod of my head I bid the others farewell and went back to the bridge.

When I got back I noticed the marines were wearing matching smirks but when I glanced in their direction they went back to a stone like expression. The princess's royal guards had a more smug look on their faces which tells me they had done this more to get their way than to ensure their charge's protection. Now that I think about it I suspect that if I hadn't told her no her guards would have gotten rather annoyed at the idea of needing a duster like me, I bet they thought it was more a punishment now for daring to defy their princess. As for the princess herself she seemed to have a look of mischief in her eyes but I felt this was more an act. She had proven her competency when King attacked and during our past conversations I got the impression of a smart and responsible young woman. Her only real fault seemed to be a child like curiosity and a bit of naviti. She hardly seems the type to use political power for something petty. I find it more likely she had a need for a ranger or perhaps just a local.

"I have been assigned your escort. I'm told you are concerned about your safety?" She looked over to her guards a moment before looking back at me. "Indeed. My family has some enemies in the British Isles and I expect they might make an attempt to disrupt our trade mission. Since this is a matter of trade I believe that this falls in the rangers jurisdiction?" Ok maybe she is just petty, that or she's a damn good actress.
"The rangers stand ready to do their duty." Regardless of her reasons I can't deny that if somebody was trying to disrupt her trade mission that would be our responsibility. Though I do wonder if the threat is real or not I don't plan on asking that to her face.

"Glad to hear it." She tilts her head a moment and her normal curiosity comes back into her eyes. "When I was speaking to the rangers in charge of customs they referred to the rangers on board as PR rangers. What does that mean?"

"There are three classes of rangers. Those working at customs are none responsive rangers, rangers who don't leave whatever station they are assigned to. The ranger's you're probably more familiar with are the emergency response rangers who are more akin to first responders. All of the rangers currently aboard are prepared response rangers, we are the ones that get sent in on missions where an immediate response isn't needed or would otherwise be impractical." Though it is unfortunate that our designation saddles us with the short hand PR rangers. Makes us sound like some poster boys or something.

"And here I thought all rangers were just rangers." We are.

"If I was you I'd not say that in front of rangers." VIP or not you're not likely to get away with a comment like that.

"Don't mention ranger designations. Got it. Anything else I should know?" I suppose I should be kind.

"Don't eat any of the meat planetside. In fact if you can you should just take your meals up here." She looked at me with some confusion.

"Is there some kind of problem with the meat produced here?"

"We don't have livestock. All our meat comes in through merchants and this year has been a poor year for trade." She still looks confused so I continue. "Most of the meat for sale right now would be recycled." It takes her a moment to understand that before looking rather alarmed.

"Don't tell me you eat people!?" Why are you so surprised? Not like Mars is a fertile landscape.

"Meat is an important part of the human diet and we already recycle the dead for various things." Leather, food, tools, and all kinds of other things can be made out of a dead body.

"You're a cannibal?" She took a step back as she said that and I noticed the marines and guards had subconsciously put a hand on their weapons.

"No. Ranger's get food and other supplies from the domes as a form of payment for the services we do." And if we didn't specify that human meat doesn't count then they'd only send us the human meat.

"I see… Mars sounds like a rather harsh place to live." What the hell kind of place did you think it was?

"Did you think it was all gumdrops and rainbows?" Our forefathers may have had better morals but ethics doesn't put food on the table.

"The information I had painted a rough frontier. From what you have told me though it's a tremendous achievement that we have a colony here at all." Spoken like a true diplomat.

"The life of Martians aside… Is there anything I should know before your meeting with the brits." After a moment of contemplation she answers. "We're not meeting with the british. We're meeting with the C&D guild." Well that could be interesting. "You mean the Colonies and Dominion guild?" She looks somewhat surprised to hear that I know their name, something that should set alarm bells off for her.

"That's correct. They contacted me while we were en route here, they are hoping we'd be willing to deliver food and medical supplies to them directly." Oh dear. "I'm gonna advise you to always deal through the domes." For god's sake just meeting with them would give them more political clout then they know what to do with. God forbid they actually make a deal. "According to Martian law I don't have to trade through the dome's administrators. Of course I already checked with the governor and he just said I would have to use facilities owned and operated by those I wish to deal with." And since the dome owns all shuttle facilities, aside the one maintained by rangers, that means dealing with him and him alone. "If you understand the dome's position on the matter I assume you plan to cancel the meeting." Unless you want to screw with the Brits anyway, I'm sure they'd love to have one of their most vocal critics suddenly gaining political power. Now that I think about it I guess there is a real threat to her life.

"Of course not. I already told you they want medical supplies and food. It may not be the most profitable deal around but it'll make a lot more than trading with the governor. Have you seen the tariffs on the dome's shuttleports? Going by ground is the only way we'd be making profit." Going by ground?

"Are you planning on trading with them outside of the dome?" Her face told me that she thought that was obvious but I ignored her past that. I was already messing with my radio to call up Nishi. She would be able to handle intelligence far better than I could and she'd do it faster than if I asked my questions to command.

"Abelus? I assume this isn't a social call?"

"Afraid not. The princess in charge of the Argonaut is planning to sell some goods planetside." It took her a moment to respond but when she did she sounded annoyed.

"Oh? Send over the details and I'll see what I can get you. I hope you realize I'll be alerting the higher ups."

"Good." Command needs to know about this.

I give her the details I can over the radio and she sends a data dump to my hud. The Shinobi 10 wasn't made to handle data dumps, or much of anything involving the hud aside from simple suit commands and the radio, but it can handle simple text only information. Even still I know the suit will need to purge the data before the day is out. The suit may be able to receive text information but it has no storage capacity for it, so I read and reread the data she sends me so as to commit as much of it to memory as possible.

Organisation: Colonies and Dominion Guild
Designation: Political
Location: Lower levels of the United Kingdom Dome, they do have a single building on the upper levels.
Purpose: A native born governor, or at the very least a governor who is from one of the other nations a part of the dome aside from Britain. Other objectives include; equality, freedom of press, an abolition of tariffs, free trade, and the right to own and operate shuttles.
Threat: No danger to trading operations, despite claims by local police. During a ranger lead investigation it was found that they had some radical elements that were purged.
Procedure: Informants are embedded in the organisation and are keeping a look out for a return of radical elements. Until otherwise stated current procedure is limited to surveillance.

"Why the hell are they making deals with earthlings?" Communications may not be heavily restricted but I highly doubt some royal family would accept a call from some random dusters.

"I'm contacting the ranger in charge of their observation now… I got a reply… According to our agents, no members of the guild have been in contact with anyone outside of the dome." Which means either our agents are incomptent or the leaders of the guild are keeping this close to hand. No ranger I'd ever met has been inept, jackasses a plenty but those lacking skills tend to die before causing any trouble.
"We won't be getting much out of them. If the guild is keeping their card close to their chest they'll sniff out anyone dumb enough to go looking."
Intelligence, as cautious as always.
"Living up to their department's motto."
"Boldness in caution. They'll keep their ears to the ground but they won't go digging for gold just yet." That'll have to do for now.
"Thanks. Do you have any ideas about the situation?" I hate going in blind.
"This isn't their MO. If it was just a PR stunt that would be one thing. I'll try looking around to see if anyone looks like they're getting ready to receive a shipment." Only thing that can be done I suppose.
"Good luck."
"Same to you." No kidding.
"J2? A word." I look around to see one of the princesses guards looking at me. He motions to the door to the bridge and after a moment's consideration I decide to humor him. Odds are he just wants to lay down the law and make sure I know

who's in charge of protecting the princess. Once outside of the bridge he turns to me and I notice his old age. From the look of him he must be around forty or so but with age therapy, a practice more or less exclusive to Earth, he could be well over a hundred for all I know.

"I'll not pretend to like you, duster. You and yours are little more than beggars and certainly not worthy of the princesses attention." He seems to be enjoying this though I note he's a bit too relaxed for this to be the lecture I had been expecting.

"However I will admit that you rangers know how to fight and seem to have a commendable grasp on your duties." He fiddles with an emblem on his chest for a moment, his eyes come up to meet his best guess of where mine are before he continues.

"I don't like the idea of going planetside. This whole thing smells like a trap and I know me and my men will be at a disadvantage once we leave the ship. I was wondering if you would have any recommendations on security." Oh? I pegged him and the other guards as stock up 'elites'. Guess they take their responsibility seriously after all.

"Where's the meeting?" He visibly relaxes and comes to a parade rest, obviously more comfortable giving information as if he was in a briefing room.

"Our meeting is at a landing pad roughly ten miles out from the dome. Nothing fancy, just a landing strip where the shuttles can unload cargo. The dusters want to meet with the princess there to hand over payment in person and get a photo to commemorate events." Sounds nice. A photo of an earthling coming down to deliver food and medicine would be a great ad. Still, a spaceport ten miles away from a dome?

"I see why you don't wanna go down there… You'll need suits. Anyone wanting a fight out in the dunes will need one and if it's a suit fight you're gonna want a long range and armour piercing rounds." After a moment I decided to return his honesty.

"I'll be blunt. Few people fight in the dunes and if it comes down to it the rangers have very few people skilled in that terrain." He looks surprised to hear that.

"You're telling me you don't train to fight on your own ground?"

"We're not soldiers. Every ranger has training for search and rescue, both void and planet, but fighting on the surface is incredibly rare." He looked annoyed but I gave him some hope.

"Lucky for you I have experience on the matter. Not too much but enough to know what to do. Of course I will advise you to request that the meeting happen anywhere else. If it's in the dome that would make things easier." Of course it would be ideal if the meeting never happened but I'm sure if anyone wanted the whole thing called off it would be her guards. This whole thing reeks.

"I see this situation is worse than I feared. My men and I did our best to train for suit combat but that was all for void combat. Never thought we'd go to the surface." Oh?
"So this was a sudden change of plans?" He nods.
"The meet up was. I had been under the impression that it'd be on the Argonaut but the princess… Well it is a guard's duty to guard, and it's the princesses job to do what she thinks is best." The man seems content with that arrangement but that doesn't mean I have to be.
"Well I'm no guard. I'll request the meeting be moved to a more secure location." And I'll look into this shuttle pad. I don't recall any shuttle pads outside of the domes, at least none that weren't owned and operated by rangers.

We go over security details for a few moments more but when he leaves I don't waste time in contacting Nishi and appraising her of the situation.
"Impossible. Legalities aside there is nobody around that could build a shuttle pad that isn't in the employ of the domes or us." And yet one was built within spitting distance of a dome.
"I doubt the earthling would fall for a fake landing zone, so somebody ordered its construction." Somebody who could keep that hidden as well.

"You think the governor had it built? That could only harm his position. Unless…" Unless the governor wasn't planning on keeping it around.

"Is it possible the governor set this up?" She takes a few minutes to reply, most likely running the odds in her head.

"It would be beneficial if one of his most vocal critics were declared terrorists. He could swope in and wipe them out then go after anyone else he thought would be a threat in the name of security." Sounds like a solid plan, aside from the risks.

"This sounds like one hell of a risk. Last time a governor tried messing with trade outside of their dome it didn't go so well." That conflict saw the rangers set above the governors of Mars and I don't think the powers that be would forget about it.

"Not much of a risk really. If he's just given funding to the guild through back channels then it'll be hard to prove his involvement. Logic isn't evidence in the court of law, and if we want to accuse a governor we'll need more than a bit of evidence on our side." Why can't everything be as simple as combat?

"I see. Well if he is involved I'll make sure to pick up some evidence…"

"Make sure you live long enough to report your findings. Dead rangers don't give much information." Boldness in caution.

"Don't worry, I'll make sure to write a report after I wrap this up." Though I said that with confidence I can't help but wonder how true that statement is. On one side we have the argonaut and a princess of Nord, while on the other side stands a governor of Mars appointed by one of the most powerful nations on Earth. If those two factions butt heads then surely Mars will suffer no matter the outcome. The question now is which side will harm Mars the least if they win, for that is the side the rangers will find itself on sooner or later.

CHAPTER 2
STORM

10/21/2300

The princess and her guards looked refined in their suits. Unlike mine which bore the scars of countless missions theirs shone brightly with new metal and glossy paint. The guards had adopted a rust like color to their suits, probably an attempt to conceal themselves on the deserts of Mars, while the princess had a suit of pure white. I don't recognize the suit's designs but given their bulk I would say they were all made to have extra armour and maybe even a separate protective layer for its wearer. This extra armour seemed to weigh them down in gravity environments, an amusing sight to be sure, but if their newfound slow speed bothered them they didn't say anything to me about it. If anything they seemed to move with confidence, a sign that tells me more than I need to know about their abilities. I'd be willing to bet they're all proud that they can use their suits at all, but I wonder how deep their training went with their suits? I suppose the question is mute at this point however, we're past the point of being able to fix that and worrying about what you can't change will just lead to needless frustration.

I was about to turn around and get on the shuttle we would be taking down to the surface when all of a sudden the metal guarding the visor of the princesses suit retracted into her helmet, followed by the tinted visor clearing up to reveal her face. Her eyes were filled with excitement and her face seemed almost flushed with joy at the prospect of adventure. At this show I concluded that this whole meeting was probably due to her sense of curiosity overriding her common sense.

"Are you ready for lift off J2?" I look over to her and nod slowly.

"I am. Your guards have thoughtfully helped me with stowing my equipment." And when they heard I was bringing a month's worth of food and water for the lot of us they simply pointed to the similar stash they had already packed in. Still brought some extra food and water for me but I was nevertheless reminded that these were royal guards and they were certainly as prepared as they could possibly be.

"So they said. You and my guards seem to share caution like a pair of wet nurses." She seems amused with her joke but frankly I found the comparison rather apt, not that I feel the need to tell her that.

"If you are ready, then let's be off." We all find seats along the sides of the shuttle and I notice that the seats must have been fitted for the suits that they're wearing. This being the case I feel like a child in an adults chair for the first time, my feet slightly dangling in the air.

As the shuttle lifts off and begins flying down to the surface I instinctively look to where there would normally be a viewport. Apparently the earthling value security, or hull integrity, more than we do as they have nowhere for me to get a look outside. How unfourant. With my view obstructed I am left with my own imagination and find it a dim replacement for the real thing.

"Breaking the atmosphere now." I notice the other's suits tense at that. It was clear that they had very little experience with reentry and I take note of the number of them that take this time to check their restraints. To my amusement I find the princess putting on the crash netting that will more or less lock her in place.

"Your first reentry?" She looks over to me, her visor clear again, and I notice her face flush slightly.

"Yes…" Oh dear lord. If she wasn't some VIP I'd be having a field day with this.

"Well there's nothing to worry about. So long as we don't slam headlong into the planet we'll be good." She nods as if that's sage advice, her main concern being her webbing at the moment. I wonder if I was like that during my first time… Oh well, nobody alive to ask about it anymore.

"Reentry complete. Landing zone in… What the hell!" The shuttle yerks to the right quickly and I glance in the direction of the cockpit.

"Missile trailing us… And gaining." Oh lovely. Getting up from my seat I walk over to the back doors and press the button to open it.

"What the hell are you doing!?" I glance back and see one of the guards undoing their restraints.

"Dealing with the missile." Or preparing to jump to safety if I can't. Once the back door was lowered I could see the open sky of Mars, and more importantly the little ball of fire representing the missile coming at us.

"It's a Downer. Land quickly enough and it won't hit us." While my suit didn't come with much in the way of gadgets a basic magnification feature barely made the cut.

"How can you tell?" I'm staring at it, but I feel like saying that won't get the message across.

"I've seen enough in use to know what they look like." Best tool to use against suspected smugglers. Just fire and if they land arrest them, if they don't land they'll be dead and outside your jurisdiction.

"Pilot, land as soon as possible and try and get us close to the dome." I ignore the others for a minute as I scan the surface for any sign of the ones who fired the missile. It was strictly a surface to air missile and the range wasn't the best so who shot it must be close.

"Landing in a minute. It's gonna be a fast one so brace yourselves." There they are! Without much thought on the matter I turned off my mag boots and jumped out of the shuttle towards the distant figures who were trailing after us in a rover.
"J2!" Ignoring the earthling again I focus on my target.

The rover looks to be a four sitter and open topped, and judging from its speed it wasn't the bog standard civilian model. What had attracted my eye though was the glint of weapons coming from the passengers on board and the fact that I could make out a suspicious looking tube on the shoulder of the man in the back. The four individuals inside each wore their own suits and to my annoyance they appeared to be using Shinobi 10s, though theirs had been painted a pitch black that probably suited the name better. It also loudly said 'not rangers' and given our exclusivity contract with Dragon Engineering I must assume that whoever these people are they are very well connected. Though I suppose that was given due to the fact that they had a rocket launcher using specialized ammo typically not found on the open market.

Some of them begin shooting at me from where they are but I was a good thousand feet above them and the fact they even bothered told me a great deal about their skills, or in this case lack thereof. I suppose they could just be excited, taking a shot at somebody who must have jumped out of the shuttle in panic once the missile got a lock. They would hardly be in the minority of people who get bloodthirsty when battle is about. Either way their efforts merely waste ammunition and for every second they continue my esteem for them falls ever further. By the time I got to a range to actually be worried about being hit I had already decided on how to eliminate them. Twisting in the air I maneuver my body and point my rifle towards the surface before firing a semi auto burst.

The momentum pushes me up and in the opposite direction, putting me on a course to land ahead of the rover. By the time I landed a few of their bullets ping off my armor so I could tell they at least weren't foolish enough to waste their good ammo. When I land into the ground I do so with an audible thump and if not for my suit I would certainly have broken my legs, and several other parts of my body for that matter, but as is I merely felt a dull pain as I rose to stand at full attention. The rover charges towards me and from the plums of sand rising around me I could tell they were shooting quite liberally at me. Thankfully while suits are amazing enhancements to humans they couldn't make you a crack shot and even an expert marksman would have a hard time hitting a target while in motion. Even still I turned so as to present the smallest target possible. Luck was a fickle mistress but if they fired at me forever they're bound to hit me sooner or later no matter the odds involved.

To further prevent myself from being shot I took out a smoke grenade and dropped it at my feet. Immediately a thick grey fog began spilling out from it and in less than a minute my vision was completely obscured by the smoke. I began to back away and as I did so I dropped a high explosive grenade primed to go off in ten seconds. Backing away, and eventually out of the cloud I began to hear the sounds of the rover coming closer. Just as I begin to think I may have gotten the timing wrong the grenade goes off and for the breifist of seconds I saw the rover as the smoke was being blown away by the force of the blast. I could see the four inside, their weapons at the ready, and noted grimly that the driver was turning the wheel as far as he could. The explosion didn't do much more than superficial damage to the rover but as I expected it had more than spooked the driver and as he spun the wheel in a panic he lost control and flipped over.

Two of them fall out of the rover, apparently not considering seat belts important when they had suits on. They rolled and flew a bit into the air while the rover continued its wild spirol. Before the two that had been flung from the rover could regain their feet

I was heading towards them, and just as one was raising his gun to me I got into close range and smacked the rifle out of his hands. I followed this attack up with three armour piercing rounds into his right leg. Normally even these rounds would take a bit to punch through an armored suit but at this range the bullets tear through the leg armour, no doubt causing serious damage to the exoskeleton and the flesh and bone under it. Immediately a mixture of blood and G-layer spill out. As he falls to his knee, presumably in a great deal of pain, I turn my focus on his friend who had come to a stop not too far away from us.

He aimed his rifle at me but he was clearly still disoriented from his crash and his shots went wide. After switching my ammo to explosive I shot a burst at his body. Two hit his chest and the third took a nice chunk out of his shoulder. The shots to the chest tear small chunks out of his armour but none of them draw blood, the shot to his shoulder however blew out a bit of gore along with the metal and he dropped his rifle to clutch at his wound. Unfortunately for him I only had need of one prisoner to answer questions and so I sent another burst into him to finish the job. The next three tear open his chest and fall back from the force of the attack. With him down I turn my attention to the man still clutching at his leg.

He would be a nice prisoner, but keeping a hold of somebody in a suit would be a real pain. Oh well, no choice but to be a little rough. I take a moment to switch to armour piercing rounds before sending a few shots into their arms. While the risk of death does increase substantially even a person in a suit won't be putting up much of a fight if their arms are riddles with holes. After they are suitably crippiled I look over to where the rover had come to a stop. The driver was dead, his body twisted at too much of an angle for him to possibly be alive. His passenger seemed to be alive, at least moving slightly, but his suit looked heavily damaged. As I began to approach them I noted the numerius inditasions on the surface showing me the horrid details of the crash.

It seemed to have flipped a good two or three times before coming to a rest on its side. The engine was still running but all the contents of the rover were gently falling to the surface. The still living passenger seemed too far gone to notice my approach, and after a quick analysis of their suit I figured they likely had a concussion and a broken arm. They'd live so long as they hadn't suffered any internal damage but frankly I couldn't care less. Putting aside my rifle I take out my axe and cut out the rover's seat belts before tossing the wounded in the back. It takes me a few minutes to drag them into the back and strap them in so while I do it I call over to the princess and her guards.

"Have you landed yet?" It takes a moment for a reply, but after a few seconds I hear a frustrated man. "Yes, and we're being pinned down by snipers. We've got two men down and the pilot isn't responding." So two teams, one to ground the shuttle and another to keep them pinned.
"I just took out the ones that fired the missile. Give me your position and I'll deal with the snipers." As I say that I drag the driver out of his seat before taking his place. The man I was talking to gives me his rough position and after a little back and forth I get an idea of where they are and, more importantly, where the snipers are. With their rough location established I begin driving in a straight line towards where the snipers are.

It takes me a few minutes of driving and for a moment I think I may have gone the wrong direction. Just as I begin to turn the rover around a loud bang draws my attention to the hood of the rover that now has a nice chunk missing from it. While putting the pedal to the metal I duck down just as another shot removes the head rest I was using. I duck down a little more as another shot rattles the vehicle.

"Is that you J2!?" I hear the man's voice over the radio and I guess they could see my little joy ride. "Little busy." As I responded I moved the rover to try and face the snipers but it was a rather difficult task when I couldn't see above the dash. Another shot must have taken the wheel as I suddenly lose control and go into a tailspin, for a moment I manage to catch a glimpse of two black suits resting on a dune no more than thirty feet away. With my targets in sight I forget about controlling the rover and decide that if I make it through this I'll remember that guarding the princess is not as boring as I would have thought.

The rover comes to a stop with its side facing the snipers, just ten feet away from where the snipers were now clearly visible. I didn't wait for the vehicle to come to a complete stop before I dove out of my seat and took cover behind the not more than slightly damaged rover. Taking out my rifle I blindly fire at the sniper's position while moving towards the front of the vehicle. My fire pins them down and when I reach the end of my cover I rise to my full height and charge towards their positions while firing at the hip. None of my shots do any harm, or even have a chance of harming the snipers but that was something they didn't seem willing to risk. In the time it had taken me to charge they had moved behind the dune and were no doubt waiting for me to crest over it so that they could shoot me down.

Instead of charging blindly I stop and take out a grenade. One, two, three, grenades up and over. I wait till the last second before charging over the dune, just as the grenades begin to go off. When I get over the crest I see the two snipers moving away from the dune and heading towards a rover that had been hidden under a tarp. One of them throws off the tarp while the other points his rifle towards me. He fires and a bullet flies past my shoulder, missing me by an inch. I returned fire, sending six high explosive rounds into the man who shot at me. He goes down as his body is rocked by the miniature explosions that blew fist sized holes into their suits before reaching their soft human flesh below. His friend chooses to flee and dives into the rover. I fire a few rounds into the rover but to my sugrin the man escapes with little more than surface damage to his vehicle. Before he could get out of sight however I moved over to his forgotten comrade and grabbed their rifle.

I'd never been partial to sniper rifles before, not being particularly useful in my line of work, but I was more than confident in my shooting skills. I take it and rest it on my shoulder, feeling the weight and recalling the class on marksmanship. Making sure to keep an eye on my target I steady my breath while I line up the shot. He was going all out at a mad dash and had made it roughly a thousand feet away. After making sure my target was lined up I pulled the trigger, even through the exoskeleton I felt the rifle kick back into my shoulder. My shot finds its mark, as I see their head explode into a fine red mist. The rover continues moving forwards until it hits a dune, where it then moves over it and out of my sight.

"Snipers eliminated." I hear the voice of the man I had talked to earlier come back over the radio, his tone now filled with relife.
"Good. We'll send out a few men to secure the area and check the shuttle. Try and hurry back, don't want to be separated if more of them show up." And I should contact command… Shit.
"Pull your men back, storms coming."
"What? I'm sure some dust storms won't bother us too… My god." No doubt he had gone outside the shuttle to take a look at the wall of sand suddenly coming our way. It looked to be a good ten minutes out but I wouldn't be the first one to overestimate a storm's speed. As I begin running back to the rover I try to call up ranger command.

"This is Abelus Fiderius, ranger currently a part of team Juliett, to ranger command. Please respond." The radio is filled with static but I can barely make out a voice.

"Confirmed… Cat… Advise digging in…" God damn it. I switch back to the channel the guards gave me as I hop into the rover.

"Can the shuttle lift off?" It takes a second for the man to respond and now I could hear the trace amounts of panic entering his voice.

"Yes, we're starting her back up now. How quickly can you reach us?" Not quick enough. As I had feared I'd misjudged the storm and it was heading towards us far faster than I could have guessed.

"Lift off immediately and break for space."

"We can see you now! We have plenty of time to…"

"If the storm gets too close the sand will clog the engines. Lift off while you can and get to safety." It takes a few seconds but I see the shuttle beginning to lift off. As it does I pull over behind a dune and begin searching the rover for emergency supplies.

"J2! I've instructed the pilot to swing around and pick you up, be ready for us in… Just do it!" I hear the princess speaking, practically yelling near the end.

"Negative. I'm already preparing a shelter for myself and the prisoner. Continue on your course to safety and I'll meet you after the storm blows over." If I managed to survive of course.

"We're losing connection with you… Can you still hear us J2?" The princess sounded concerned so I did my best to fill my tone with confidence.

"I can hear you. Please inform ranger command of my coordinates as soon as you can." The sooner a rescue party can be formed the higher my chances of survival.

"…" I looked up from pulling out a tarp and saw that the storm was already beginning to envelop me. Thin lines of dust are being carried over the ground on the wind, like the breath of some great beast, and I knew I would not enjoy looking over the crest of the dune I was hiding behind.

I do my best to secure the tarp to the side of the dune, burying one side of it in the dune itself, before pulling the rest of it down and over the rover. Normally the rover would have a sealed compartment that would make this easier but as is there was only a thin piece of metal over the middle of the vehicle and it did little to keep the tarp above where I and the prisoners would be taking shelter. After a brief moment of consideration I decide to secure the other end of the tarp to the tires of the rover, leaving the side facing the dune alone. Before I seal off the rover entirely I shove the prisoners into the small gap between the dune and the rover. Then after climbing in I secure the tarp the best I can and get on top of them.

Cramped as hell and far from ideal, but the best I could do in the time available. As the storm gets closer I not only hear its roars but begin to feel the vibrations in the ground. Sand from the dune shakes onto us and for a moment I think it may crumble under the weight of the storm. Thankfully it holds, but the same could hardly be said for the tarp. Trace amounts of metal and rocks tear through the tarp at high speeds, slamming into the rover and sending shrapnel around us. Thankfully we were safe from the worst of it in our little hole but I heard the pings of metal on my suit and covered my visor. I doubt the suit would break whatever was hitting me but the same could not be said for the visor. It was the weakest part of any suit no matter what the designers did to try and fix that and in a storm it was the weak link that would cost me.

In this case however it seems I should have done more to prepare. When I felt pressure on my chest I moved my arm away from my visor and saw to my horror that the tarp was slowly falling onto me from the weight of the sand being shifted over it. The tarp straines to hold it and as I watched sand began to pour in from the holes that had been made in it, filling the rover and beginning to drip onto us. The tears began to spread and soon the tarp started to fray at the seams and I knew it would give out soon. I should have taken the time to flip the rover on its side… Oh well. All I can do now is hope that the sand doesn't crush us. At least if this is the end I can die knowing my mission was a success, and that my body shall soon be one with Mars. An honor that was slightly dimmed by the fact that my tomb would be shared by the prisoners resting under me.

Well I suppose I should take this time to get comfy. Soon whatever position I am in will be the position I stay in until either I'm rescued or die. I do my best to get comfortable but surprisingly it was rather hard to get comfortable on top of two suits while being sandwiched between a dune and a rover. When the tarp finally gives and the sand pours in to lock us in our final positions I had just managed to get moderately comfortable. As I slowly adjusted to the fact that I could not move an inch nor see anything the thought finally came to me that this would be a very painful death. I could not drink nor eat so in three days I will die of thirst, a particularly gruesome way to go. The idea of slowly succumbing to thirst does little for my state of mind and I feel the first stages of panic come on.

I do my best to hold myself together however as I know if I start to panic the only thing that will happen is that I run out of air before water… Now that I think about it, thirst was a far off danger for now, air was of more immediate concern and I should begin rationing it now. I calm my breathing and do my best to enter the zen like state rangers use when on long deployments in the void. It takes a while but soon I manage to enter a calm state of mind, but for how long I'll be able to maintain this I have no idea. I suppose the only thing left for me to do is wait and hope that rescue comes soon.

Chapter 3
Salvation

10/23/2300

I was woken from my sleep by a disturbance in the sand above me. My whole body could feel the sand above me shaking violently. Is it possible that the storm is still going on? My suit's clock says it's been two days now, but storms could last for weeks if they were bad enough. Of course a storm like that wouldn't have escaped notice so I doubt this shaking is a result of one. A flare of hope comes through me as the realisation comes to mind. This shaking must be the result of somebody shifting the sand around me! The shaking continues and soon something strikes my right leg. As soon as it does the shaking suddenly stops and I feel something grab my leg. This is followed by a slow and tedious process as those who have found me begin to carefully remove the sand above me.

This was a procedure I was uncomfortably familiar with and I knew that finding somebody was normally easy, the hard part came when you had to dig them out. A deep penetration scanner can spot a suit easily enough, even through a mountain of sand, but removing that sand would take time and effort. While they may have dug out a route to my leg that rout certainly missed my head and the rest of my body. Now they would have to carefully shift the sand away until my whole body has been dug up. This was far from a quick process and hours go by as they free me from my sandy grave. When I can finally see the light of day again I let out a short cheer, careful to make sure that my radio was off when I did so.

My rescuers raise me out of my tomb and I am greeted by a half dozen rangers in Rover 3 suits. The tools they had used to save me from my grim fate lay around us, and a rover with the logo of the ranger painted on the side was waiting nearby. They led me, and dragged the prisoners, to the rover and put us in the back. After confirming we were all alive they bound the prisoners in clamps of steel and locked them to the rover. Once they were secure I figured we'd make our way to the dome but the rangers stopped me.

"The Earthlings were hoping to pick you up. Insisting in fact." Oh? I would rather go get some food though.
"Can I get something to eat first?" I could always catch a shuttle on its way up later.
"They're already sending a shuttle down to pick you up. I can call it off if you prefer." Hell no. After

learning what kind of food they kept on those shuttles there's no way in hell I'd turn them down.

"No need. I've waited this long for food, what's a little more?" As I say that I look up and see a shuttle coming down towards us.

"Your duty honors us all. I'll inform command that you returned to your post. Do you have any requests for the prisoners?" Our attention turns to the two locked in the back of the rover.

"I'm sure intelligence will know what to do with them. Just make sure they're alive to talk." His helmet nods up and down.

"Don't worry. I'll make sure there aren't any accidents on the way." Or he'll do his best at any rate. Rangers can be trusted to do what's best for the whole but seeing others using our suits, to attack our own no less, was testing our restraint. To be honest I wouldn't even complain too much if I was told the prisoners didn't make it, but duty required me to at least attempt to secure their safety. Besides, if they live they can suffer punishments befitting their crimes.

"See that you do. I'm sure the mines could use two strong workers." And considering their crimes they'd never be leaving those mines.

In the time we had been talking the shuttle had gotten closer and was now coming in for a landing. The rear ramp came down and I nodded to the ranger I had been talking to before making my way over to the shuttle. Inside I find a couple people who introduced themselves as doctors. As soon as the ramp closed and the shuttle was sealed they asked for me to leave my suit so that they could examine me. I had no reason to refuse and after exiting my suit they looked me over and asked me several questions regarding my health. They also took a sample of my blood and ran it through some tester they had on them, before finally allowing me to rest. The first thing I did was go over to one of the overhead compartments and look for food. After scrounging around for a little while I found some emergency rations, nutrient paste and some vitamin pills all washed down with a bottle of water. Far from the lavish meal my body seems to demand but more than enough for me at the moment. I knew from experience that eating too much would simply make me sick.

After I finish eating I look over my suit. It had taken little damage in the fight but the storm had not been kind to the paint job. It's rust colored paint now looked pale and it suddenly looked several years older than it was. I traced a finger over an area on the side where a different type of metal had been sanded down to match the rest of the suit. Not long ago that had been the blade of an axe that had caught on the exoskeleton of my suit. At first we were planning to take it out and fill it in when we landed on Mars but I had decided that I would keep the blade in as a reminder of my failure to keep an eye on my surroundings. The job had been one of haste and it hadn't looked good but the storm had cut away at it and the baking sand that had been on top of me had done a good job of making the different metals blend. I'm sure Ishii will not be impressed when she sees it but I rather like the look.

The shuttle pilot's voice comes over the intercom and they alert me that we will be landing soon. The doctors strap themselves in and I enter my suit. When the shuttle comes to a stop and latches itself down I feel the sudden change in gravity as the shuttle's artificial field is replaced with the Argonaut's. The feeling is odd as it always is but at this point in my life I have done this thousands of times and while I note that the doctors wobble slightly as they walk I exit the shuttle normally. When I get down onto the hanger deck I take a look around and take in the familiar sights before moving on. The doctors follow after me and we part ways after a short while. They were no doubt looking forward to returning to their medical ward while I continued on my way to the bridge.

Once I make my way onto the bridge I see the marines and the guards giving me a look mixed with a hint of respect. This caused me to pause for a second, as while I had grown used to all manner of looks from Earthlings I can not recall a single time one had given me a look of respect. Fear, anger, hate, disgust, distrust, relief, and even gratitude, but never have any earthlings looked upon me with any kind of respect. The princess also gave me a look filled with respect and perhaps a hint of satisfaction as she motioned me over to her. I came towards her and her guards, many of whom had only recently stopped instinctively putting a hand to their weapons, gave me nods of approval.

"A pleasure to have you back J2. You had us worried when we lost contact with you." I nodded towards her.

"Sorry for the inconvenience. I hope your experience on the planet did not hinder your negotiations." She gives me a grin before taking out a datapad and handing over to me.

"We had to meet up here but the deal ended up being heavily in my favor. Apparently they were concerned we'd think they were trying to kill them and were willing to pay a whole lot more than we thought they would." So I see. The guild is apparently willing to pay top dollar for Nord medical supplies and food.

"Congratulations." This was certainly a good deal for her and her kingdom. The guild may be paying more than they want, god only knows where they plan on getting the funding, but if they can come through this deal would be a great benefit for both parties. Nord gets a tidy profit and the guild gets more medicine and food than they'll know what to do with.

On the surface the deal ended there but I knew what would come. The guild may have paid an arm and a leg but they still paid less and got more from Earth than they ever could from their own dome. They'll start opening shops and stores soon and selling their products at a price that undercuts their competition while still earning them a profit. In the short run they'll suffer but in the long run they could end up becoming quite the business. I still have no idea why a political group would enter into the trading game but now that they're in it I'm sure the answer will come sooner or later.

"It went so well I was able to offer a little more on other trade deals. Quite a high demand for wood apparently." Yeah trees are a bit scarce on Mars. One day one of the terraforming projects will work out... Maybe.

"Good to hear. I suppose you will be trading with the other domes as well?" She nods, a somewhat predatory grin on her face.

"Until the dome's administrators lower their tarrifs I don't plan on dealing with them at all. Thankfully the guild's efforts have inspired others. This time next year there will be hundreds of shuttle pads littering mars just waiting for us…" Something tells me she made some exclusivity deals. Also did she say hundreds? As in hundreds of shuttle pads will soon be operating god knows how many shuttles?

"I suppose we'll need to increase recruitment." Her grin looks a bit more friendly as she regards me. "We'll keep you in business for as long as you keep us safe." She sounds rather happy about that but I hope she's not expecting this kind of protection forever. The only reason we're on board her ship is because of the high value targets we suspect will attack her.

"If nothing else you've kept us entertained for a little while." At that moment my radio beeps to inform me that somebody was trying to contact me directly and I back away to my normal spot.

"Yes?" I heard Nishi's voice filled with amusement, and knew that something good, at least in her mind, must have happened.

"Our contacts in the guild recently gave an interesting report. Apparently an anonymous donor not only paid for their shuttlepad but also directed them to a cheap and discreet construction company. While you were napping intelligence has been having a field day." Well good for them. I'm sure they enjoy the chance to prove their worth as much as the rest of us. "And have their inquiries met with anything of note?" "I wouldn't be calling you if they hadn't. The company is a front for some smugglers we've been looking for for nearly a decade. The information we found when we raised them is worth its weight in gold. Drop off points, inside contacts, sellers, buyers, supplyers, friends, and rivals. We got it all and more." Sounds like a surprisingly well organized criminal venture.

"Anything on why they'd want to kill an Earthling? Or how they managed to get their hands on some of our suits?"

"The suits were easy enough to trace back. Dragon Engineering was very helpful in this regard and it didn't take us long to find a corrupt factory manager making a little extra on the side. As for why they were targeting Nord's trading delegation… All we can tell is they were hired by somebody who knows how to remain anonymous. The only clues we have is that they're rich and have connections with organized crime." Not much to go on, but something about this made me feel uneasy.

"I don't like this. Smugglers don't often make good hitmen and this wasn't a target they could just walk away from afterwards." Nishi clicks her tongue.

"You should have been in intelligence, your mind would have been put to better use. Whoever ordered the hit either had the money to make it worth it, or they had the power and influance to make not doing it suicide." I muse over that information for a few seconds.

These smugglers have been working on Mars for at least a decade and must have made quite the network for themselves. Whoever got them to do the job knew about this network but had to have been too powerful for the smugglers to just kill. Considering the equipment they were able to get ahold of that limits the amount of people that could have that kind of pull to a select few. Pirates would be my first guess but a smart smuggler, which this group must have been to last so long, could get the rangers to deal with them. Hell it would hardly be the first time smugglers have traded information on pirates they'd pissed off for their freedom so I don't see pirates being the answer. That leaves only one other option.

"I don't suppose the governor has displaced some of the tax revenue." Nishi lets out a short laugh before answering.
"Took you less than a minute to guess our primary subject. I'm telling you, you should really join intelligence. You'd make a great field operative."

"I'm too trigger happy for that kind of work. Have we got any leads on him?"

"Not enough to justify raiding his manor. He recently 'donated' a large chunk of change to several groups, all without giving his name of course." Of course.

"Is it possible to trace the money back to the source?" I knew the answer of course but had to ask to be sure.

"No. Our only chance of getting more information is capturing somebody who knows what we need to." Which would be the ring leaders. They'll be the hardest to catch but if anyone could do it they'd be working in intelligence.

"I wish intelligence luck in their hunt. Keep me informed?"

"Of course. We in intelligence pride ourselves in our ability to work with others." And get others to work for you of course.

"Thank you. With any luck this whole thing will be wrapped up before I get back." That way I don't have to get involved. While I'd enjoy seeing one of those high and mighty governors fall I know all too well what kind of consequences that would have. Riots in the streets would be the least of our problems and no matter how bad the governor may be the next one could be the devil's own.

"I wouldn't worry about it too much. You have far more interesting things to worry about at the moment." That is certainly true. Once the Argonauts voyage resumes we will have to fight the Queen and the Doomrider. Both dangerous predators of the void, both soon to find their end by our hands.

CHAPTER 4
THE QUEEN'S PLOT

11/13/2300

Ever since we entered the section of space intelligence thought the Queen would attack us we have all been on edge. Most pirates got by on cunning or pure boldness, but the woman called the queen of pirates is a cunning foe. She started her career by taking several ships by convincing them she and her crew were inspectors. After people got wise of this trick she tricked them into thinking she was a part of the military and that she was ordered to inspect ships for contraband. As her career took off the ways she tricked her prey into allowing her on board their ships only expanded to the point that now it would be suicidal to accept any ship's offer to dock with them. In just ten years of operating she has put more stain on the reputation of the rangers and the coast guards of Earth than any other pirate in history. Only the Doomrider could cause us more discomfort and the fact that he would be attacking us after the Queen was not lost on us.

In this regard we envied the Earthlings. This was their first voyage and while they knew all the tales of the Queen's cunning they thought them no more than cautionary tales. None of them seemed to take her reputation at face value and while we pressed upon them that she was every bit as dangerous as they had been told only the marines seemed to take the threat seriously. They doubled the number of personnel at their posts and now all of them had their full kit on at all times that they were on duty. Marines in suits now regularly walked the halls on patrol and the checkpoints on the ship all now had heavy weapons in place. The crew themselves had also been taking lessons in firearm practice and I noticed a few of them now carried sidearms on their person. It was clear to me that the Earthlings were on guard, even if they didn't take our words as seriously as we would like. The crew was as ready as it would ever be and to be frank I fear that if we pushed any further they may stop taking the situation seriously at all.

However, as I settled into my place on the bridge I felt particularly on edge. My gut told me something bad was happening and as the man in charge of communication called out to the princess I got the feeling that things were about to go wrong.

"Your highness! We have a message from a satellite just outside of our range." Thora looked over to the man and nodded towards the screen on the bridge and soon a video came on. The woman on a golden throne looked down at the camera, somehow making it look like she was far above us.

"Greetings children of Terra. If you're receiving this transmission it means you've already entered my little trap. I would recommend you give up as frankly I find little gain in battle. If you don't turn off your engines within the hour I will of course take your ship by force. I hope you make the right choice." From her tone she didn't care one way or the other but I knew the truth in her words. Her career was clear on the point of her always allowing those who surrender to be spared, and she had on occasion just left her prey alone if she thought the battle would be too costly.

"Dozens of contacts at extreme range… Thirty… Forty… they just keep coming!" The princess looks over with surprise and then her face pales at the number of ships heading towards us. For a moment I was also stunned by the mere numbers of enemies, then my common sense came over me.

There is no way in hell that many ships would be under one person, the pirate who had the most ships was the king and he was dust, so that means that most of these must be fakes.

"Lucas, the queen is spoofing our sensors." It takes a second for him to respond.

"Understood. I've relayed the information to A1 and he wants us all ready to deploy." Hardly a bad call. If we can take control of one of the real ships then we can hack into their sensors to find their friends.

"Where are you all going?" One of the marines asked, his question drawing the attention of the princess and the other members of the bridge crew.

"The queens showed her hand. We'll take her ship and relay their sensors to you." The Earthlings muttered at that and the princess shook her head. "What good will that do? Our sensors are working just fine." I shook my head as we headed out of the bridge. I don't have time to explain everything and the longer we delay the worse our situation will get. "Just have your weapons ready and your communications link open. You'll find out if you have anything to worry about soon enough." Hardly the best way to communicate to her but we really need to get going. The bridge was the farthest away from the hanger any of our teams got so the whole operation was waiting on us to reach the hanger. Even as we run down the halls as fast as we can go we're still the last of the teams to have fully assembled and the others are already getting aboard their shuttles. While I got onto our shuttle I noticed the Earthlings around the hangar were giving us odd looks and a few of the marines were saluting us as we moved out. I wasn't sure how to react to them so I simply ignored them and focused on my fellow rangers. Once we were all loaded up onto the shuttles A1's voice came over the radio.

"Ok boys and girls, time to bag us another big one.

The bitch may think she's smart spoofing our sensors but she's over played her hand. Odds are there are about a dozen ships around us escorted by heaps of junk putting off enough heat to look like ships, those we don't have to worry about. Our primary objective is the Queen's Voyage, which has been identified directing ahead of us. Board her and secure the target. Her fellow ships, real and fake, will scatter once their leader is out of the picture. Any questions?" Nobody asked any and so after a moment we were all on our shuttles and preparing for take off.

The ride was tense to say the least. While we all strongly believed that most of the ships on our sensors are fake that doesn't change the fact that we were charging towards a larger vessel that we had almost no information on. The Queen's Voyage used to be a large merchantmen but after years of modifications and restructuring only the crew aboard her could tell you the layout. If this was any other pirate we could just land, plop a mine on her hull, and leave. The Queen was a wily one though and as such command wouldn't accept anything less than a positive identification of her body. Which meant boarding her flagship and praying that she was actually on it. We would hardly be the first to board the Queen's Voyage, but none of the previous attempts had done much and the one that managed to reach the bridge reported that she had never even been on board.

If she wasn't on board this whole operation would be a bit of a bust, but at the very least if we secured the ship we could figure out which ships were real. Their sensors would have the data to tell which of the ships were junk or not and once we got that information back to the Argonaut they could deal with the real ones. Worst case scenario, that the Queen isn't on board and that the ships were all in fact real, we could turn the Queen's Voyage on her allies and cut a hole for the Argonaut. Well I guess the worst case scenario would be if we all died but if that came to pass none of us needed to care about whether or not the ships enveloping the Argonaut are real or not.

"Coming in for a landing. Prep for…" Suddenly the shuttle jerked and a beam of pure light cut through the top of it, cutting a molten trail of metal where the roof used to be. We backed ourselves against the walls of the shuttle to avoid the molten metal as it fell to the floor. The metal quickly cooled as the coldness of the void seeped into the shuttle but for a moment we all played a very real game of the floor is lava. "How the hell did they detect us?" Demipho sounded rather calm considering the seat he had hastily vacated now had a pile of slag on it. "Who cares about that. Let's get the hell out of this coffin before they get another hit." Norma was a bit less calm but her frustration was more than understandable.

"Landing in ten! No further signs of fire from the Queen's Voyage." What? If they had detected us they should still know we're operational.

"Could they have guessed where we'd be coming in from?" Natasza sounded almost impressed but I didn't have time to ponder her question as the shuttle came to a jarring halt.

"Everybody out! Find a hatch and start breaching." Lucas was the first out of the shuttle's main hatch while Demipho and I took the doors on the sides of the main compartment. We all got out of the shuttle as quickly as we could, and a good thing as suddenly lasers suddenly began carving it up. The pilot was forced to bail out but before she could her body was cut in two by one of the many lasers now carving up the shuttle.

"Enemy laser emplacements! Focus fire…" Lucas's voice was cut off as his left arm, which had been pointing towards a team operating a laser cannon, was seared off. He fell to a knee and clutched at the stump that used to be his arm while the rest of us opened fire.

The situation was bleak to be sure. Our shuttle had landed along with several of the others on the side of the Queen's Voyage, and all around us were heavy weapons teams with laser cannons at the ready.

Unlike our void rounds, which couldn't easily penetrate a suit, their laser cannons made short work of the armour we had put our faith in. Several dozens of rangers were cut down or otherwise dismembered by the weapons and all of our shuttles were torn to bloody pieces. In return all we seemed able to do was scuff the paint on their suits. The only one of us who could do any real damage was our lancers and they had been priority targets. Demipho had enough sense not to open fire as soon as he came out of the shuttle but the moment he did he would be lit up by lasers. Unless of course they had other concerns.

"Demipho! I'll distract them, cut a path for the rest of the team while they're busy with me." I don't wait for an acknowledgement, I know he'll do as he's told and I have faith that the team will break through this kill zone and help the others do the same.

I undo my mag boots and send myself flying towards one of the laser cannons. Immediately one of his teammates fired at me and I began to float away as their bullets propelled me into the void. Before I was propelled away however I managed to toss a grenade and to my immense satisfaction it gently smacked into the barrel of the laser cannon before going off. The explosion was far greater than I had expected, no doubt setting off the generator powering the laser, and the people manning the weapon disappeared in a bright light that tore a crater into the ship.

Two of the other cannons that had been dealing with other teams suddenly shifted their attention to us but before they could fire one of them was hit by Demipho's lancer. While it didn't explode with the same violence as the first one it was reduced to a pile of junk and the man operating it now had a hole in his torso the size of a dinner plate. This left a gape in our environment and none of the rangers needed any encouragement. The wounded were picked up and carted along while a rear guard was left behind to buy time for the rest to escape. In all this confusion I was left alone long enough to propel myself behind another heavy weapons team and were busy tearing apart our rearguard.

I buried my axe into one of them and as the others reacted let out a bitter laugh. They had so happily gunned us down just a moment before but now I had an idea to get some payback and I would not be denied! The rest of the team attempted to fight back but I had the element of surprise and without their precious laser they were left with the same void rounds we had so ineffectively used. In mere seconds they were all dead, their bodies still mag locked to the ship but their blood and G-layer floating out into the void. I didn't take the time to admire my handiwork and instead focused on manning the laser cannon.

The thing was a bulky contraption and the wires connecting it to its massive power generator normally demanded several people to make sure it worked at peak performance. I however didn't need to care about such things. All I needed to do was turn the damn thing and while I would have loved to be able to adjust the power useage and the like I settled for merely being able to slice through suits like a hot knife through butter. When I lined up my targets I pulled the trigger and with immense satisfaction cut the bastards to ribbons. The laser made a long stream of death that I simply had to turn to turn a little to cut down a whole weapons team, and with this power I made short work of several of them. My vengeance was cut short when another laser cannon suddenly fired in my direction. It was a badly aimed shot but I got the message and before they could lower the deadly beam I walked away. The stream continued downwards and destroyed the cannon I had been using. I saw the beam however over the generator just before an explosion blinded me.

Instinctively I turned off my mag boots and the force of the blast sent me sailing down the side of the hull. I had to use my axe to slow me down before locking my boots onto the ship again. It was then that I realized I had gone very far off course, nearly flying into the main engines. I did notice a maintenance hatch however and began heading towards it. While I made my way there I called over the radio to my team.

"Lino can you read?" I waited for a moment but all I got was static. Looking over to the part of the hud that showed me the life sighs of my team members I noticed it was gone. My suit must have been damaged and lost connection to the others, and my communication systems must have been hit as well. That or something was interfering with the signal. No matter. I was on my own anyway and all this has done is cut off any chance of a quick reunion with my team. After I enter the ship I will be able to make my way to them sooner or later.

Making my way to the hatch I take a moment to take apart the control panel and begin fiddling with the wires. While not my normal role in a breach I was familiar enough with the process to have the door open in under a minute. Virgo could easily have done it faster but I'd settle for this. The hatch opened up and I quickly made my way inside. I had to do the same thing again to get through the airlock and to close the hatch but after just a few more minutes of wire slicing I was stepping into the ship.

While I have no way of knowing the layout all ships have roughly the same general layout. I had entered close to the ship's engines so the main maintenance bay will be somewhere close by. The bridge though could be anywhere and given our landing the idea of splitting up and quickly overwhelm resistance is no longer an option. The others will most likely enter the ship and try and stick together. On the bright side the loss of all our shuttles means that we don't have to worry about securing an escape route, though I doubt command will look so fondly at the loss of all our combat shuttles. The loss of assets aside I need to come up with a plan.

Taking the bridge solo isn't an option, even if I managed to surprise them I would surely be overwhelmed. Another option now is to try to regroup with the others but that would be rather difficult given I have no idea where they entered the ship and only the vaguest of ideas of where I ended up. In the end my best option is probably to find something to do that would support the main group. Just roaming around killing anything that moves will draw attention away from the others but that's assuming I don't run into something that can deal with me. I suppose I could try and screw with the engines… That would warrant an immediate response that could buy time for the others. Diffantly better than skulking around like a chicken with its head cut off. Putting up my rifle I made my way through the ship's hallways in the general direction of the engines.

Before I got too far away however I heard movement heading towards me. With no place to hide I move up to the end of the corridor and wait for whoever is coming to pass by. As their steps get closer I try to count the number of people coming by listening close to their footfalls but before I can even take a guess the first one comes running straight past me. By instinct I grab the man by the scruff of his neck and toss him back down the hall he came down. I hear several cries of confusion and when I look at them I notice most of them are armed with shock staffs and have cuffs on their hips. They must be guards of some kind, but what they might be doing I neither know nor care. All that matters is that they're pirates and none of them have weapons that can harm me.

Given their lack of weapons able to pierce my suit I pull out my axe and get to work. The first one goes down without a fight but the next one tries to block my blade with their staff. Unfortunately for them the axe was made to cut through far tougher things than a simple metal staff with electricity running through it. The shaft splits in half and my axe continues downward until it digs into the man's shoulder, cutting all the way down to his ribs before I stop it. I kick the man, now thoroughly dead, away from me and into his still surprised companions. They scream out in horor and begin to try and run down the way they had been coming but I don't feel like letting them off so easily. I charge into them and begin hacking them to ribbons with very little effort on my part. The last of them almost manages to escape into a room I hadn't noticed before but just as the door opens I throw my axe at him. The blade catches him in the back and he flies forward from the momentum of the blade.

I followed him and saw that the room he had entered was some sort of brig. Cells lined the wall and a set of stairs lead to three levels, no doubt having more cells. At the other end I saw a guardhouse where they must store the prisoners stuff as well as keep watch. Coming out of that guardhouse is a man in a suit with a large metal pipe. He looks over to me and points his pipe at me and in response I pull out my pistol with my free hand and shoot him square in the head. The explosive round blows off a chunk of the suit's armour but it doesn't appear to have finished him off as he lunges towards me with a howl of rage. I put two more rounds into his head before he fell to the ground in front of me, his helmet torn open and his skull now nothing more than white specks littering the ground. After holstering my weapons I turned to walk away but a voice stopped me.

"Ranger! Please let us out!" I turned over to see several people were lining the cells and were pushing their arms through the bars to get my attention. "You have two seconds to give me a reason to let you out."

"WE KNOW WHERE THE QUEEN KEEPS HER LOOT!" Filthy pirates wasting my damn time. I turn and begin to walk out of the room but they continue.

"SHE HAS MILLIONS IN HER VAULT! SHE EVEN HAS A WARSUIT FROM EARTH!" A warsuit? Now they're just making up shit to get me interested. No way in hell one of those things ever left Earth.

"Enjoy oblivion scum." They wasted enough of my time and after leaving the room I made sure to close the door. Last thing I need is for some random crew member to go in there and let out a bunch of their buddies.

After leaving the room I continue my journey towards where I think the engines might be. I stop at every door and open it to see what might be inside, and to make sure I don't get shot from behind after walking past, but for the most part I find crew members going about their jobs. They seem quite relaxed given the fact that they're picking a fight with bigshots from Earth and the Rangers but that soon changes when they get a look at my now crimson axe. Their screams fill the ship as I butcher them without mercy. Some of them beg, others flee, all die by my axe sooner or later. Given the lack of armed individuals this area must be close to the engines.

That or I stumbled into the crew quarters in which case it really must have been their unlucky day.

"Stop him!"
"Somebody get…"

As I got further into the ship I met more and more crew members and they had slowly begun to arm themselves. Unfortunately for them they didn't have any suits on hand at the moment and as such I did my best to close the distance with them as quickly as possible.

"Form a firing line or something just… FUCK!" I suppose I could say that they have courage. Even as I cut them apart with ease the only time they run is when they don't have a weapon to fight me. What a shame they choose this career path, I'm sure their determination would have seen them go far in any military or private security.

"Close the bulkheads before he…" Your shouting annoys me. I cut off the man's head as he looked at me in shock and horror. The rest of the pirates begin rushing towards me and dogpile me while a few begin to file out into an adjacent room. As much fun as it is to use the axe I decide that now's the best time to bring up my guns. After getting the bastards off me I level my pistol and fire at those fleeing. They fall to the ground in agony but those still moving reach for a control panel on the wall. After a moment of thought I shot it, sending a shower of electricity and shrapnel into the face of a woman that was rushing for it. She falls to the ground screaming while clutching at her face. I decided to be merciful and put a round into her head before turning my attention on the others who were trying to find any cover they could.

I'm a kind man so I wait till they have gotten behind whatever cover they could before switching to armour piercing ammo. Most of them were using desks or cabinets, tables and chairs, whatever could potentially give them even the slightest of protection. However no matter what they use the end result is the same. In less than a minute the whole room is silent and I put my pistol back on my hip. After looking around again I found that no one was moving so I continued heading towards the sounds of movement. I'm pretty sure I should be close to the engines now but I think I may have gotten turned around at some point.

"We stop him here!" A team of five men move into the room and point rifles at me.
"Drop him!" They open fire on me at once and pour an impressive amount of fire onto me. I turn to keep the pressure from building in any single spot while moving towards them. They aren't dumb enough to

let me get close however and quickly stop their attack to withdraw. One of them is a bit too slow though and it costs him a leg from the knee down. As he flops to the ground in agony the others turn and fire at me again. Three of them press their attack on me while the fourth moves up to grab their fallen comrade. The display was rather curious since pirates aren't well known for taking such risks for one another but before I can speculate further one of them gets a little too close to me and I lash out. His chest is ripped open and he falls backwards with a howl of pain.

"SHIT!" One of the others drops their rifle and moves over to the man and begins to staunch the bleeding while the others begin pulling back. Their tactics seemed to be to my benefit as they stopped firing on me to focus on their wounded. They were surprisingly good combatants all things considered but I had wasted enough time on them. I take out my rifle and mow them down in a quick burst of fire. With them out of the way I look around and see another team of them setting up at the door I was planning to make my exit. They peek out to fire at me but as they do my own bullets tear into them. The rest of their team decides now is the best time to withdraw and as they start running the other pirates that had been attempting to make some kind of defence began to run a well. I move up and find myself in yet another room that could be some kind of crew quarters. Just how big is this ship?

"Bring him down!" A few bullets petter off of my shoulder and I turn to the side before killing my attackers. Where did all those suit wearing bastards with the lasers go? Don't tell me the queen only had… Well fuck me!

I had to dodge out of the room as six suits came charging in with fucking miniguns already rotating. They sent tens of thousands of rounds in my direction in seconds but before they had the time to turn me into paste I dived through a door and found myself in a corridor with several doors lining the walls. After taking the time to drop a smoke grenade I ran towards one of these doors at random and found that it was locked. Not having the time to hack it I kept going down the line until one of them opened. Rushing in I found what appeared to be a bathroom. I didn't waste too much time thinking about it and went to the opposite side of the room and pointed my rifle towards the door. While this may not be the most appropriate place to make my final stand it would serve me well enough.

"Come in…" Just as I'm mentaly preparing myself for death I hear somebody coming over the radio. "This is J2. Your transmission is garbled, please repeat your last." The voice came again a bit clearer but it still had a ring of static to it.

"B4 here along with what's left of my team. We're being pinned by some suits with heavy weapons. Can you assist?" Suits with heavy weapons huh…

"Don't suppose those heavy weapons happen to be miniguns?" They take a second to responde and for a moment I think they may have been killed.

"Can confirm that they are indeed using miniguns. Do you have a bead on them?" Maybe.

"I just so happened to have been engaged with them recently. I'll try and help you but I make no promises."

"Good enough for me. If you can at least buy us a few seconds we can move to a better position." That I can do.

I leave the bathroom and head back to the room I had encountered the suits previously. Sure enough one of them was keeping a lookout but compared to the six that had driven me off this was manageable. I ducked back into the bathroom as his bullets began to take chunks out of the surrounding wall. After taking out a high explosive grenade I wait a few seconds before popping out again and throwing it towards my opponent. The blast momentarily envelops him and in that time I charge towards him. His weapon begins to roar out in vengeance just as I close in on him and my suit crumbles under the abuse, but I still manage to get close enough that he's unable to bring his minigun to bear on me. With a single motion I bring my rifle to his helmet and before he can do anything more I pull the trigger. A spray of explosive rounds make short work of his helmet and the head it protected. He slumps to the ground and I poke into the room and see that two of the other five were beginning to turn to face me. I couldn't handle another round with one of their weapons so I backed away as they began to fire into the doorway.

"Took one down and two more are focused on me. That's the best I can do for you B4."
"It was enough. We lost one when we made our move but we're now heading to a better position. Regretfully it looks like we can't meet up with you at the moment."
"Figures. Don't suppose you've found the bridge?"
"Somewhere near the center of the ship from what we can tell. What's left of us is heading there now. Minus your team, they're trying to secure the hangar two decks below us."
"Thanks. I'll be heading to rejoin them as soon as I can."
With that we go our separate ways. Engines or stairs, which one will come first?

As I continue to wonder the halls I begin to hear the sounds of battle ringing off the halls. Things were getting intense here for sure, a shame so many of us got taken out in the landing. Still if we can find the Queen we'll be able to put an end to this whole thing. Just as I'm thinking that I ran right into a man that was leaving a room. Since he wasn't in a suit he ended up bouncing off me and landing with a sickening crunch. I looked at where he had come from and saw a few people wearing a type of kevlar armour and carrying rifles.

"F… Fire!" One of them cries out and the rest do as he bids.

Instead of risking some of their bullets penning my suit, especially since it's taken a bit of a beating already, I decide to move back a few steps to the side before quickly tossing a few micro grenades into the room. They bounce around before exploding, sending a shower of shrapnel into those inside. Their kevlar keeps them safe from the worst of it but any exposed parts of their bodies are now bleeding from numerous cuts and scrapes. This was fine with me since all I needed to do was buy a little time for me to prime a high explosive grenade. When that goes off the kevlar does little to hold back the sheer force of the blast and those close to it are flung around like rag dolls. Those that were far enough away to escape with just superficial wounds were too dazed to even notice me as I walked in and gunned them all down.

After making sure none of them were alive I noticed a few of the dead didn't have any armour on and that there were some computer terminals lining the walls.

After closing the door I took a look around and figured that this must be some kind of secondary communication system. I suppose if I take the time I can connect it to my suit's radio and we can use it to broadcast throughout the ship. That would certainly be more helpful than hoping to find the engines or a way down to the lower decks. With that in mind I walk over to one of the terminals and get to work. Work in this case being to take out a flash drive and shoving it into one of the open ports. The moment I plugged it in the programs on the drive began the real work of getting through their firewall and decrypting any information on the terminal. Once it had finished the terminal opened up and I accessed its systems.

To my surprise the terminal seems to be set up with quite sophisticated systems. Most of the systems seemed geared towards remote hacking as well as… As well as connecting to FTL transmitters and using them to access other systems remotely. That's some pretty expensive toys the Queen's messing with. Wonder what she wants access to. With more than a small amount of curiosity I select one of the transmitters and a wall of information comes on my screen. Ship readings… Familery ship readings…

Unless I'm mistaken this is giving me live access to the Argonaut! How the hell did they manage to get something like this on board without our notice? Well no matter how they did it they did it and it looks like this is where the overwhelming number of hostile ships is coming from. They weren't using junk or spoofing our sensors, they're actively changing what the Argought is seeing. Even better they knew we were coming because they had access to the hanger's camera feeds.

I turned off the program that was making the extra ship's appear on the Arhonauts sensors before sending a message to the captain's personal terminal warning about the transmitter. To make sure she understands it's from me I signed it with my name as J2. I also informed her not to wait up for us. Now that our shuttles are all destroyed we would win or we would die, no other options remained for us. If we won then we could steer the ship over to them or take a shuttle back, and if we died then there was no reason to stick around here. To my surprise she responded rather quickly, telling me that the Argonaut could easily take a single ship so we should focus on escaping. I was about to send another message when I realized there was no reason I couldn't just call her using the terminal. After messing around with a few of the programs I had an image of the Argonauts bridge and could see the princess and her guards looking at me with their mouths agape. It was then that I remember that I have been cutting a very bloody path through the ship and probably looked rather worse for wear.

"I am afraid I don't have much time to talk. The Argonaut should continue on its voyage and leave these pirates to us." We could hardly have it said that the rangers needed others to rescue them from pirates.

"Are you suggesting we abandon you again? This time with the rest of the rangers that have done nothing but aid us so far?" She shook her head in annoyance. "I will not allow it. Already I have stained my house by abandoning you once, I shall not do so again a hundred fold!" She seems determined, and now that I look at the others they also have a similar look of determination. Seems that their pride wouldn't allow them to just leave. Fools.

"Don't let your pride…I appear to be out of time." Turning around I point my rifle at the door just as it's kicked open. Two guys with suits charge in with miniguns leveled. The first one takes three explosive rounds to the head and drops but the other turns their weapon on me. I dive to the side and a shower of bullets trailed after me. As I roll to my feet I bring my rifle to a rest on my shoulder and press the trigger back as far as it could go. Rounds explode all along their suit as they turn their gun on me and my own is suddenly pelted by thousands of rounds. It proves to be too much abuse for my suit and I get alerts that it has been breached soon after he began to land hits. Before my suit is entirely destroyed, and me along with it, I manage to damage his visor. With his vision suddenly impared his aim takes a nosedive and his shots go all over the room. My own shots stayed accurate and soon he joined his comrade on the floor. With them dealt with I turned to the terminal and raised my rifle.

"Sorry for the interruption…" I took out a repair kit and began to put on some patches.

"Are you ok?" All things considered I don't feel like that answer warrants a response.

"I need to get back to the fight." And away from this room, more of them were bound to come and I don't think I can survive another encounter with a minigun. Hell at this point I don't think my suit can handle even low caliber rounds with its normal immunity.

"Shouldn't you go to the rear and recover?" Yeah one of the handful of rangers left standing should take this time to find a place and hide.

"No." After saying that I head over to the terminal and yank out the drive. The princess seemed like she was about to say something but as soon as the drive was extracted the terminal went back to way I'd found it, nice and locked.

After I put away the drive I head out of the room and

resume wandering the corridors in my quest to find the stairs or the engines. Though I guess at this point finding the engines was rather pointless. Even if I found there was no way I was in a condition to pose a serious threat to it. Whoever is guarding it should be able to handle me now that my suit had been whittled down so much. That left finding a way to the hanger the rest of my time was attempting to secure. Seriously where are all the ways down? Shouldn't there be stairs or a… DING… an elevator… I turned to the small room filled with people who seemed relieved to be away from wherever they were moments before. Their good cheer ends the moment they see my rifle. Perhaps I should have waited for them to leave the elevator before killing them. Now I had to step on them to get inside and the whole place was covered in blood. Oh well. I get inside and hit the button for the floor two levels down.

Before I reach the bottom level I try to contact anyone within range but all I get is static. Before I would have said this was clear evidence of jamming but given the current state of my suit I can't rule out my radio was damaged in some way. Guess I'll just have to trust that no ranger would mistake me for a pirate. And then the doors slide apart and I find myself being shot by a ranger with one arm. Lucas's bullet glances off my shoulder, his aim adjusting at the last possible moment, but I still felt quite the punch.

"Nice to see you too Lucas!" They lower their pistol
and I wait for his reply. A minute later his voice
comes out of the suit's speaker.
"Your radio fragged?"
"Apparently."
"Well then get to the hanger. Just down the left here.
We got a repair team fixing up what they can and our
medics are hard at work as well. Thomas and Lino
will get you back in shape once you reach them."
Good to know they're both alive.
"I'll make my way over there. Oh and I managed to
make contact with the Argought. Their sensors are
clear of hostiles except this ship and they insist on
coming to pick us up."
"How kind of them. I'll inform B2." B2 is in charge
now? Hopefully there was still somebody in Alpha
team to pass the torch.

With nothing more to say I make my way to the
hanger. Once I reach there I see a butchery. The
fallen had been collected and moved here but not for
safe keeping. Their suits had been taken of them and
were now being used as spare parts for the repair
team. Looking at them I could see that the repair
team consisted of those who had lost limbs or were
otherwise impaired due to battle damage. Even in
their current state they did their duty and were

repairing several ranger's suits. As I got in line to have my suit patched up I looked over to the rows of dead and tried to see if any of them belonged to my team. Unfortunately, or perhaps fourantly, I couldn't make out their faces from this angle and the few that I could were lacking in that department now. When my time to get fixed up came a ranger looked me up and down before grabbing suit plates and welding them on me. It was an ugly rush job that would have to be fixed properly later but for now it would do the job.

Once I was done getting patched up I went back to Lucas. The repair team hadn't been able to fix my radio so I had to return to him to get my new orders. Once I got back to him he simply informed me to guard the elevator with him. I did so without comment and just pulled out my rifle.

"According to Delta they're about to breach the bridge now. This whole thing will be done in a few minutes."

"What happened to Bravo?"

"B2 got caught in a crossfire and not much of his team was left to begin with. And before you ask Charlie is currently laying in the hanger." Well that's just great.

"A high cost. One that could have been avoided."

"What do you mean?" I passed him the drive.

"Somebody put an FTL transmitter on the Argought.

Knew we were coming as soon as we began loading onto the shuttles."

"Then we'll have to talk to the Earthlings to see which one of them sold us out." He sounded rather angry when he said that and I couldn't blame him. Whoever installed that transmitter better pray a ranger never finds them.

"On the bright side Foxtrot reports that the bridge is secure and the Queen has been neutralized." Downside is that Foxtrot reported it and not Delta. Don't even want to know what happened to Echo.

"Well then at least this wasn't a complete waste of our time." If we had done all this and the Queen had escaped… Best not to think about it.

"Also the repair team is reporting some marines are landing."

He sounded more than slightly annoyed at the news. "Not like we're in a position to refuse. At least now we won't have to waste as much time cleaning up the place." He turned to look at me and even though I couldn't see his face I felt the heat of his glare.

"Our blood and their glory. You and I both know that's how it's gonna turn out." Yeah… Can't really deny that. No matter how odd these Earthlings may be the rest of their kind will do the same thing they always do.

"I can see the headlines now. 'Hero Princess Leads Charge!' Bet it makes front pages." He shakes his head in clear annoyance.

"And if we're lucky they'll mention us when they ask if there's any point in funding us." I ignore the bitterness in his voice and listen to the sounds of approaching footsteps. Turning around I see a squad of marines in suits heading in our direction. They stop when they see us and one of them, with a red cross on the front of their helmet, motions to Lucas. "Head back to the hanger and we can treat you there." Lucas motions to the elevator we're guarding and shakes his head.

"Guarding the elevator. Not like you can regrow limbs anyway." The medic looks over to another marine, a sergeant by the stripes on their suit, before nodding.

"If you insist. When you get back to the ship though, go see a doctor." After that the squad moves off. They must be securing this deck before moving on since they ignore the elevator completely.

While we were still guarding the elevator the action was pointless now since soon the place will be swarming with marines. Still though we guard it until the rest of the rangers come down, the fallen laden between them. Even with the marines taking over the clean up we spend hours combing the ship for the dead and wounded. To our disappointment there were far more of the former and by the time we had gathered all the rangers in the hanger, both alive and dead, it had become apparent that we were a shell of our former numbers. Surprisingly the marines seem more shocked by our losses than us. Whenever they entered the hanger they couldn't stop from glancing in the direction of the rows of our dead. I guess they had to be wondering where we plan to put them all, something I myself had been thinking about. I guess we'll have to settle that with the princess. Ideally she'd allow us to send our severely wounded, in this case those missing limbs, back with the prize ship. I didn't think she'd refuse but she'd be well within her right to demand we stay with her ship given our agreement. Well whatever she decides to do I know I'll be sticking around for the final leg of the journey. A good thing too since I had a score to settle…

CHAPTER 5
LOOKING TOWARDS THE FUTURE

11/14/2300

The princess looked over us all with calm eyes but I could tell that she was not in the best of moods. My time with the Earthlings gave me an idea of how they think and I knew her mind was not on the success of the operation but rather on the losses we took. A waste as the victory was worthy of the sacrifices made to achieve it. There was no reason to mourn for those who died doing their job, especially when that job was so important. Taking out the Queen will encourage trade to Mars and thus more felth will flow to the dooms. Even if we had all died the only thing we'd have mourned was that we wouldn't have a chance to take down the Doomrider. But we still stand, and what's more the princess not only allowed us to send our wounded off with the captured ship but she even let us keep all looting rights. All in all the mood among the remaining rangers was rather festive and before sending off our wounded, Lucas among them, we took on the job of using up as much of the food and alcohol to send them off.

The Earthlings for their part don't partake in the celebrations which leaves us time to discuss our situation over a nice dinner. As Lucas would be leaving us soon I took up the mantle of team lead a little early and took part in the discussion with the other team leaders. The battle had whittled down our numbers and we needed to reorganize. First though we had to go over who was left.

Alpha: four members.
Bravo: three members.
Charlie: zero members.
Delta: six members.
Echo: one member.
Foxtrot: five members.
Golf: Seven members.
Hotel: four members.
India: zero members.
Juliett: eight members.

That left us with thirty-eight active members to protect the Argonaut. Far too few to do the same plan we'd had before. Thankfully we knew our current oppoinet well and wouldn't have to waste manpower defending the engine or crew quarters. Doomrider always goes for the head, killing the bridge crew and anyone that gets in his way in such a brutal manner as to terrify the surviving crew into submission. Of course that was assuming he and his men bothered with tactics and didn't just decide to spread out and paint the interior crimson. Each and every one of them is a drug filled berserker in battle and a dangerous psychopath when they're not. Thinks like pain, remorse, and fear just don't register in their minds. On paper the best tactic in dealing with them is to force them into kill zones but in practice no one has ever managed to contain one of their boarding forces. The best anyone has ever been able to do is survive long enough to be put into irons before being sold on the slave market, assuming the bastards didn't keep them for their own amusement or pleasure.

Still we had hope. The marines were competent and there are plenty of choke points to thin the herd. Our primary problem is how to deal with Doomrider himself. Unlike his mob he takes a cocktail of drugs that drives him into a frenzy but also lets him retain his faculties. What's more if the rumors are to be trusted his cocktail gives him inhuman reaction speed, as if everyone around him is going in slow motion. Some even say he can dodge bullets but so far no evidence has presented itself to back up these claims, nor has any come to deny them. The only thing we could say for sure about him was that nobody had ever beaten a boarding action lead by him personally nor has anyone ever survived a fight with him. He is a man to be respected in battle and one not to be underestimated.

Given our assets we really had two options. We could secure the bridge and pray that the mob doesn't decide to butcher the crew, or we could draw them into a massive battle somewhere nice and open. Once they get into a frenzy the lust for battle will overcome many of them and if we started a battle early on we should be able to contain them. Problem is that if we fight them that way they'll be able to make the most use of their numbers. Hundreds of blood crazy lunatics in suits aren't just going to be contained just because we want them to be. When we attacked the Queen she had every advantage at the start and we still overcame the ambush, our current adversaires should be able to do at least that given their track record. What's more they won't be cowed by lasers or any other weapon we bring to bear. The only way to deal with them is to kill them and killing a man in a suit is hard enough at the best of times and in this case it would be a man in a suit built for battle with its wearer hyped up on drugs. Wounds that would drop a normal man, even in a suit, will just annoy them.

After discussing it for a while we agree that both plans have their merits and both will require heavy cooperation with the marines. As such we will need to get their approval before we go any further. With that realization it's decided that I'll bring both proposals to the princess and have her decide which we'll follow. Before doing so however I make sure to eat my fill and have a few drinks with the team. In particular I find myself talking with Lucas over a game of cards.

"I heard they wanted to give you an artificial arm." He let out a grunt as he laid down two cards before drawing two more.

"Bunch of mother hens is all they are. I'll get a proper replacement once I get back to Mars." I suppose if there's one thing Mars is good at producing it's artificial limbs. Given the high need of them among our miners and rangers it's no surprise the industry flourished.

"Are you going to take your retirement?" Like all rangers he was entitled to retire after losing a limb in the line of duty. If he didn't want to completely retire he could always take up a teaching post or transfer over to a support position.

"Nah. I like being a prepared response ranger too much." As he speaks I place down three cards. Man what a bad hand…

"I'm surprised. Figured you'd take this chance to open a bar somewhere." He glances at me in mild interest.

"A bar? Really? I like drinking too much." But if you owned the place I may get a free drink or two.

"Fair enough." I lower my hand and wait till he does the same. As I had suspected his hand beats mine easily and he smiles in triumph.

"My win! At this rate I'll be getting that money I gave you back." Thank god for prize money or that'd have hurt.

"It'll be mine again before the end of the night." Even sooner if you keep drinking like that my friend.

"Perhaps… Oh? Is that the princess I see coming over here?" Are you really trying to get me to turn around so you can peak at the deck? If so, you're gonna have to come up with a better lie.

"Is she now? Then she can watch me earn back my paycheck." I say that as I deal out cards to him, making sure to shuffle them thourily.

"Ignore her at your peril man. She seems to be heading this way though." Stubborn isn't he. Three aces huh?

"Place down your bet already." He shrugged and threw down his cards.

"I fold." COWARD!

"Damn you."

"I expect your payment when you get back to Mars. Now I'll leave you alone with the princess and her guards." Would you stop bringing up… Oh what do you know she is here with her guards.

"Hello J2… Or are you J1 now?" She looked tired but her eyes still glinted with curiosity.

"Spare me. Last thing I need is a promotion to team lead." I do enough of that when I'm working with IR.

"If that's your wish. I was wondering if you could tell

me who's in charge of you all now." I wonder…

"F1 is the woman you're looking for. Afraid she's already turned in though." By that I mean her and the rest of her team are passed out in the corner. I get the burden of command is heavy but the least she could have done is stay conscious.

"Where can I find them? I have something I need to discuss with them." Oh that isn't happening. Better put on my diplomat cap on.

"If it's nothing urgent can I handle it? In fact I had been told to talk to you about our new deployment." She looked at me and for a moment I thought she would refuse but then she nodded.

"You've lost your shuttles. I know the ones you had been using were a bit more specialized than the ones we have but if you need them you're free to use them. Captain Erichsen also asked me to relay his request to talk about defending against borders." That's all? Well that makes things easy.

"Odds are we won't be using your shuttles. The last target isn't going to be using too many large ships, if any. I'll be more than happy to relay the plans we've been working on though." She nodded, but her eyes seemed downcast. I motioned for her to say something and she obliged me after a moment of hesitation.

"We were dismissive of the theatre before. Even after we were boarded none of us thought for a moment that we'd lose. But when our sensors were filled with enemy ships for the first time I thought we might fail. For the first time I thought about what might happen if we failed. I will admit that it has shaken me in ways I couldn't imagine." Must suck to have a leader so arrogant that they never even wondered what would happen if they failed. Something tells me that saying that wouldn't help much.

"Little late to start worrying about failure so you might as well start planning the victory parade." Though something tells me she already has. Those that never wonder about failure tend to have an idea of what will happen after they succeed.

"I suppose you're right. We shall have much to look forward to once we return to Nord. My father will likely claim it as one of the greatest achievements of our generation. Erichsen will probably be promoted and we'll all get the classic hero's welcome. What about you? How will you all celebrate once you get back to Mars?" I shrug and motion to the party that was starting to wind down.

"This with less beer and no fresh food. After that the others will go to their designated domes and begin looking for replacements while I go back to emergency response." Her head tilts in mild confusion, the same way that it always seems to do when she's about to let curiosity get the better of her.

"Doesn't sound like much of a celebration, and certainly not one worthy of your efforts." Seems like fair recompense. Not like we've done anything above the call of duty.

"More than we need. Besides we've had better food on this endeavor than I've ever had before." She seemed satisfied about that and nodded.

"Well then I'll have the cooks prepare a grand feast to send you all off." That actually sounds rather nice.

"We'll be looking forward to it."

CHAPTER 6
DOOM

11/30/2300

When we'd first entered the asteroid belt we'd all been tense. Ships had to go into them to reach the numerous mining bases dotting the belt and once a ship entered the belt their sensors would begin to be riddled with interference. Something is always there to mess with the ship's sensors. Be it mining equipment, the numerous stations, or the asteroids themselves. To make things just that more interesting the belt left little room to maneuver which left the Argonaut as a blind sitting duck. It was the perfect place for an ambush.

Yet nothing happened. Even as we began to fill the cargo hold with raw ore there was no sign of the Doomrider or any other pirates. The closest we got to a danger were when we needed to steer through tight corridors of asteroids where straying too far in any direction would ram us into one of the massive rocks. The pilots certainly felt the tension though it wasn't for the threat of being attacked by pirates. They had enough on their plate making sure the ship didn't crash. Thankfully they all seemed up to the job and nothing so much as scraped the hull. Still, as we began to leave the belt with our hold filled to the brim we all began to wonder when the hammer would fall.

Just as we began to leave the belt, with the safety of open space in sight, the alarms began to blare. Hundreds of shuttlecraft began to pour out from behind asteroids and in tight confines of the belt we couldn't bring the lasers to bear. The missile pod opened fire but it was clear that it would do little more than dent the numbers coming at us. Doomrider would make his landing but he would not find us unprepared. Both marines and rangers worked hand and hand to lock down portions of the ship and secure the strategically valuable parts while not leaving the crew to fend for themselves. Marines took control of the cargo bay as well as the hangers while rangers guarded the engines and bridge. As always my team stood on the bridge but now we had been joined by the remnants of Echo, Alpha, and Delta. A full half of the remaining rangers. The other half joined up with marines in the engines. As for the crew, they were locked into the medical ward with the marines too wounded to be of much use elsewhere.

It was hardly a solid defensive line and the brunt of the fighting would be left to the marines but there was nothing else we could do. I looked back at the princess and her royal guard, now in their suits, and saw them staring at the overhead display. The dots representing the enemy shuttles blinked in and out of view. The interference was bad enough that several missiles lost contact with their targets and disengaged as their safety protocols took over. Those missiles that hit their targets though left nothing in their wake. Every missile that connected with their target took our one of the many dots on the screen, but there were still far too many dots coming in and out of view. For our sake I hope that most of those dots are just the result of the interference messing with our sensors but deep in my gut I knew that most of them were real.

When the first of them clamped onto the hull I heard the crew mutter curses under their breath. A report came in that breaches were being detected on all levels. Just a few moments more and the sounds of gunfire filled the ship as the marines met the borders. They engaged them at every choke point in the ship but many positions were left hopelessly vulnerable as new attackers would breach behind them. Sections were lost very quickly but in all cases the marines were sure to enforce a heavy toll on their killers. If the pirates cared they didn't show it, lost as they were to their combat drugs.

Thankfully the majority of the attackers didn't seem concerned with taking the engines or overrunning the now mostly cut off cargo bay and hanger. It was clear their target was the bridge and to get there they had to pay a steep price in blood. The elevator and emergency stairs were vital choke points that the marines defended with great valor. Unfortunately for them no amount of bravery could overcome the sheer ferocity of their charge. All it took was for one section to fall and then the whole line crumbled like dominoes. The marines were forced back to the bridge and the force currently outside acted as a rearguard for them. While their comrades joined us on the bridge they began to fire at the incoming horde. I saw the laser turn and fire and knew that an uncountable number of people must have just died from that single action, but just as I thought that the man operating it was riddled with bullets. Even as he fell another marine took his place.

Just as the marines in the bridge began to rally the ship was rocked by an explosion and the marines in the hall were engulfed in fire. The fire didn't stop there and surged towards us, stopping short of the marines who were seeking cover behind our suits. The front of our suits grew red hot and I felt the interior of the suit heating up. It was very uncomfortable but I managed to focus on the threat at hand. Men began pouring onto the bridge before we could close the blast door and our rifles cut them down as quickly as they came.

Their blind charge was fear inducing to many who cried out in terror but the line held firm. Tens of thousands of rounds poured into them the moment they entered our line of sight and no amount of combat stimulants could keep a man going after being reduced to so much red mist. Still though I saw many examples of the effectiveness of the drugs they used. A man whose arm had been blown off still charged towards us with no regard for their lost limb. Another who was bleeding from what seemed a thousand wounds appeared unaffected by the amount of blood lost or the bullets still tearing his body apart. Most horrifying of all though are their eyes. They'd been utterly drained of their humanity and were filled with a fiery rage that seemed to engulf their very existence. It was then that I realized that we weren't fighting men. These were nothing more than deranged monsters that had only a passing resemblance to humans. It made me sick, that man could stoop so low.

Casings soon filled the bridge and my ammo was starting to run low. When I ran out of conventional rounds I switched to void rounds, then armour piercing. Soon I was using up my precious high explosive rounds and while they made short work of the men attacking us we would be at a disadvantage if we were attacked by suits. I said as much to the others but there was little we could do. If we stopped firing we'd be overrun and if we didn't stop we'd be left open to heavy infantry… Just like they want. No matter what we choose it's ok for them since the ones in charge will have it easy either way.

"This is annoying." As I said that I was about to toss a grenade when I realized how dangerous that would be. If they were to kick the grenade back it wouldn't do us much harm but many of the marines behind us only had basic armour. A careless grenade here could do far more harm than good.
"I'm running low on ammo over here!"
"Same!" The marines were calling out to each other, and I noticed in my peripheral that some of the bridge crew were now passing out fresh magazines from several large bags the marines must have brought with them. Perhaps ammo wasn't as much of

a problem as I thought?

"SLAUGHTER THEM ALL!" Suddenly I heard a voice echoing through the bridge. A large heavily armoured suit standing at least seven feet tall charged onto the bridge. Following after him are several others in suits but none could compare to their leader. The suit, black as night, came rushing towards us and I grinned. The Doomrider had arrived and it was time to collect his head.

"Primary target on the bridge." A calm voice said over the radio. All the rangers present immediately shifted aim and soon high explosive rounds were tearing chunks out of the blck suit.

Before we could finish it at range however it closed ranks at a speed almost beyond human comprehension. A great axe that I hadn't even noticed suddenly appeared in the monster's hands and with a single swing cut a member of Alpha in half. The attack was so sudden that it stunned the rest of us for a second. How could he move so fast in such a bulky suit? By the time we came to our senses two more members of Alpha were dead at his hands and the other suits were closing in to provide support. None of us needed to communicate with each other. Every ranger turned their full attention on the Doomrider and left everything else to the marines and the royal guard.

As I made my way to assist the last living member of Alpha raised my rifle and fired at the Doomriders back. Several solid hits blew small craters into their suit but it didn't seem to have any affect on him. With hardly a care in the world they stepped forward and cleaved the last of Alpha like he was nothing but an insect. I felt my blood begin to boil but now was not the time to lose myself to anger. We formed a semicircle around him and began pouring our remaining HE rounds into him but just as it looked like we were going to bring him down, rifles began to go silent. One by one we all ran out of ammo for our rifles and then the Doomrider made their move.

He surged towards as we were all dropping our rifles and reaching for our axes or sidearms. The last of Echo and two of Delta were dead before I had even taken my axe and pistol out. Before I could charge a loud blast reverberated throughout the bridge and I looked over to see Demipho had fired his Lancer. The shot took the Doomrider in the side and a large hole the size of a dinner plate was blown clean through. Normally this is where they would fall over dead but the Doomrider was no mere man. He turned on Demipho and in a flash was in front of him. As he brought his axe down to kill him I moved in and barely managed to shove my teammate to the side. I moved to raise my pistol to their now exposed head but found my arm was suspiciously absent.

Instead of shooting him in the face several times and bringing this fight to an end I instead sprayed blood all over the front of their suit.

They didn't seem bothered by it over much. Their axe came back to finish the job by again a loud crack went out and another large hole was ripped into the Doomrider. Again this didn't seem to be enough to kill him but it was enough to move them back just a little. A good thing as their swing that would have certainly cut me in two merely sliced a line through my chest plate. Not even my exoskeleton was able to slow down the blow and I took a couple steps back. At this point my vision was starting to fade and I knew my time was fast approaching its end. I would almost certainly die here but before I leave this world I'm taking this monster with me. The others were already stabbing into his back and flanks while Demipho was lining up another shot.
I rushed into the fight and raised my axe up high. Just as he waved his axe in a wide arc that caught several rangers I attacked. My axe slammed into their armpit and I knew immediately that it was stuck. He tried to move his arm down but my axe prevented him from fully lowering his arm. This left him open for several more attacks from us and a final shot from Demipho seemed to do the trick. He began to sway back and forth but even in this state he was dangerous. He dropped his great axe and his left arm came to smash

into my head. His fist wrapped around the front of my helmet like I was a child and he began to squeeze. My helmet began to crack and soon my visor began to splinter. The radio filled with the voices of my team only to be cut off as my helmet's internal systems were crushed. This bastard…

I had no gun nor even my axe but I still had one weapon on me. Before my helmet gave out I ordered it to spit out a HE grenade and take it with my final hand. With the last of my strength I shoved the grenade under his chin and cried out with all my heart.

"JUST FUKING DIE!"

The explosion blew off his head and my arm from the shoulder down. He went limp and I slid to the ground in a heap. Somebody dragged me away but at this point I was barely aware of what is going on around me. The sounds of battle were still present so we had not won yet but I knew I was no longer a part of this fight. Even if I wasn't about to die of blood loss I still didn't have any arms on me to fight so I was truly worthless now. Just as countless rangers before me I was left to my own end while my team rejoined the fight. To my surprise however somebody took off the shattered remains of my helmet and began treating me.

It was one of the marines, one of the ones with a red

cross on their helmet. They looked me in the eyes and started talking to me but for the life of me I couldn't understand them. Their mouths were moving but no words seemed to be coming out. Now that I think about it, the sounds of battle have stopped. Had we won? We must have if I'm being treated. The marine put something over my mouth and I suddenly felt fresh air filling my lungs but even that sensation soon faded. The marine moved out of my sight and I paid him no further mind. Most likely he had decided I wasn't going to make it and had just given me something to ease my passing. Rather kind earthlings, to waste their resources on a dead man…

*

When I open my eyes I find myself in the ship's medical bay. How odd. I'm sure I had lost too much blood. Looking to my side I see the stumps of my arms. My left was gone at the shoulder and the right at the elbow, yet I was alive so I think I came out of the battle better than most. Still this was a rather disturbing development. My arms are gone… Will I be able to afford decent replacements? I'll need advanced prosthetics if I want to continue being a ranger, they'd need to be both sturdy and dexterius. At the low end I'll be paying a year's salary and if I want to get to my former shape I'll need to pay ten times that. Hell I don't even know if some of the higher end stuff is available on Mars so I may have to pay extra to have it shipped in.

"Oh you're awake? Good. You had us worried when you didn't wake up." A man in scrubs comes into view and I see him give me a smile full of kindness. For a moment I think he's going to sell me something but then I recall that he's a doctor and is probably just happy to see one of his patents on the mend.

"How long was I out?" He looks over a datapad while he answers.

"Almost two weeks. Was wondering if you'd sleep all the way to Earth." Huh?

"Earth? I need to get back to Mars and con…"

I guess the rangers won't be missing an armless man. At best they'd put me in a training center somewhere to make use of my experience while I try and get some suitable prosthetics.

"Don't worry about it. Her highness already talked to your superiors and explained everything." As he says that he takes out a small pen light and points it into my eyes one at a time.

"Mind filling me in on the situation?" He ignores me for a moment and types something into his datapad.

"Hm? Oh right, of course you wouldn't know. Her highness decreed all those who were injured protecting us would get the best cybernetics possible. We picked up those who needed replacement surgery when we were on Mars and once we get to Earth we'll be able to fix you all up." That woman confuses me. This trip couldn't have been something a naive kind hearted young woman could have come up with yet that is how she acts most of the time. Only when it comes to business has she shown even a hint of ruthlessness but even then many of her deals appear generous. Now she takes Martians to Earth to reward us? It's too generous… Just what is that woman planning, and what does Mars have to do with it?

ABOUT THE AUTHOR

Currently working a part time job while going to college to become a high school history teacher Drew's yet to experience what life has to offer and hopes to see the world. Drew is the second oldest of six and loves all his siblings despite how much they may annoy him at times.